JUST FOLKING AROUND

GOOD FOLK: MODERN FOLKTALES, BOOK #0.5

PENNY REID

HTTP://WWW.PENNYREID.NINJA/NEWSLETTER/

COPYRIGHT

PART I

NOVEMBER 2015

"I know I walk a fine line between being a respected actor and being what they call a sex symbol."

— EVA MENDES

"We're in Mayberry. This is Mayberry. And I think the entire town is at this wedding," Lina whispered, wearing incredulity and fascination beneath her flawless application of makeup. Whatever Lina thought or felt at any given moment always shone like a marquee on her face. This made her an excellent method actress but also a terrible liar.

I didn't contradict her even though the name of the place was Green Valley, not Mayberry, and I doubted those assembled for our mutual friend's wedding reception encompassed an entire town. The white tent was full, but I wouldn't call it crowded.

Lina had arrived in Green Valley yesterday, whereas I'd flown in just two hours ago and hadn't seen anything of the town. But if this place was at all similar to where I grew up, I understood her comparison to the fictional city of Mayberry from *The Andy Griffith Show*.

"I'm telling you, the downtown is one and a half blocks by six blocks, has two hardware stores and no Sephora. It's a film set waiting to happen. I can see it now—a new quirky TV dramedy about lumberjacks and the bakers who love them, hokey and/or plucky background music included."

Grinning at Lina's description, I took a sip of my water. "Maybe there's a woodworking culture here. Don't look down on people for enjoying their wood."

"Ha ha," she deadpanned, but then smiled. "You and your innuendos are the highlight of my day."

"Are there any other kind of innuendos? Speaking of which, want to invest in my new pornographic breakfast cereal venture called In-u-end-O!s?"

She grimaced and laughed at the same time. "Please don't tell me what the shape of the cereal would be. I think I can guess."

Chewing on my straw, I winked at her, and she rolled her eyes. I always used a straw whenever possible. Even these so-called stain lipsticks fared better and lasted longer if one drank through a straw.

"Look at all these beards," Lina muttered, her eyes darting over the wedding guests. Seeming to shake herself, she sent me a look. "Oh, I forgot. You grew up in Ohio."

"So?"

"So, it's the cold part of the country. People probably have lots of beards there. It might as well be Michigan." She shivered, her wince increasing.

"Never say that to someone from Ohio. And never say the reverse to someone from Michigan." I may have left my hometown the day I turned eighteen, but the Ohioan in me—who still had the odd craving to play euchre around Thanksgiving and missed the changing of seasons—objected.

She scrutinized me. "Is this about sports? Is that why I shouldn't say the thing about Michigan?"

"Of course."

"It's always about sports with you midwesterners." Lina's gaze moved from me and narrowed at something over my shoulder.

Likewise, I glanced around the white wedding tent without focusing on any details, not wanting to commit eye contact with anyone, instead absorbing the general splendor of our surroundings. I felt a sudden, strange pang of restlessness and anxiety. Sienna Diaz had somehow achieved the impossible in her wedding décor: understated yet opulent. I was not surprised. Sienna Diaz built her brand as Hollywood's reigning sweetheart on achieving what everyone had believed was impossible.

But I hoped Sienna wasn't making a mistake. In addition to understated opulence, from the outside looking in, her rushed wedding to a park ranger from small-town Tennessee looked and felt like a big, horrible mistake.

Too late now. It's done. Poor Sienna.

With that depressing thought, and despite attempts to keep my gaze unfocused, Ana Ortega caught my eye and waved. I gave her a bright smile and waved back, telling myself to avoid that side of the room. She and I were up for the same role—a busty damsel sidekick in a Sclumicker blockbuster—and my callback was next week. I didn't want her to inadvertently psych me out. Ana was good people, but I wanted that role.

Holding up a glass of champagne from her spot across the room, Ana pointed to it and mouthed, *You're not drinking?*

I shook my head, gesturing to my water and mouthing the words, *Early flight.* My departing flight was early, but that wasn't the reason why I wasn't drinking. I never drank at industry events. My first year on the West Coast taught me that lesson quite well. It also taught me that sobriety makes other people uncomfortable, so I learned to fake being buzzed like a pro.

Ana thrust out her bottom lip, in the universal facial expression for *That's too bad.*

"So many beards . . ." Next to me, Lina's muttered lament snagged my attention. It sounded as if she found the sight of so many jawlines adorned with hair alarming.

I pretended Lina—whose back was to Ana—had said something funny, grateful she'd had the idea of being each other's plus-one. Lina and I were never considered for the same film roles, mostly because she preferred indie films that made important statements in lieu of money. But then, she descended from Hollywood royalty and could therefore afford to make statements rather than a paycheck. My mom had just recently—and tentatively—started to warm up to my chosen profession, though I think my latest film may have put a damper on her enthusiasm.

It's true. I'd been topless, full-frontal shot, arms over my head, tits filling the frame. For the record, I was not ashamed of going topless and it absolutely *was not* a reaction to my messy split from Harrison Kent. First of all, it was for work, and I'd accepted the role before Harrison had cheated on me; secondly, I loved my breasts; and thirdly, there is no thirdly. I was determined not to let anyone make me feel bad about showing off parts of my body I loved, doing a job I loved.

I just wished . . . *sigh.*

I just wished there were some way to both live my life on my own terms and spare my mom the judgy looks. She'd been through enough.

"Well, we have to do something when it's cold outside," I said brightly, turning so that I was no longer in Ana's line of sight.

Lina moved her narrowed eyes to me. "Wait? What? What are we talking about? You grow beards when it's cold?"

"Sports, Lina." I shook my head at her. "I'm still talking about midwesterners and sports."

"So, when it's cold, you go outside and watch sports?" Her eyes rounded. "That makes no sense."

"No. We sit inside and watch sports."

My friend made an impatient sound, setting her empty champagne glass down on a nearby table. "That reminds me—I've been meaning to ask, what is a toboggan?" We were standing near a tray of both water and champagne, making it easy for her to reach behind me and grab another glass.

"Really?" I looked between her and the champagne flute. "You've been meaning to ask me what a toboggan is?"

"Yes. I keep forgetting to ask. I read the word in that dog sled movie Jorge is making and—anyway, you're the only person not originally from NYC or SoCal that I know. What is it?"

I had to laugh at her. "You know you can search the internet and find answers to your most pressing questions anytime you like. You don't need to save them for me."

"Ugh. I hate the internet. There're so many people there. Just tell me."

"It's a dog breed," I lied, watching her. She was so gullible.

Lina was Ariel from *The Little Mermaid* and I was the seagull. Except, unlike the bird in the movie, I purposefully misled her with fictional explanations for the mundane stuff everyone should already know. Lina lived under the sea, in the magical kingdom of beautiful people and champagne problems.

In our odd-couple friendlationship, I was the expert on real-people things, like how to pump gas, drive cars that weren't Teslas, use physical keys to unlock doors, and how to interact with non-touch-screen tech. She'd once encountered a rotary telephone like the one my great grandma still insisted on using. I'd convinced Lina—for ten minutes before setting the record straight—it was a device for Morse code that sent telegrams.

"A dog breed?" Lina nodded thoughtfully. "I guess that makes sense ...?"

"No, it doesn't make sense because it's not a dog breed, Lina." Now I was laughing for real. "If you want to know, stop being lazy and get thee to the internet."

"Just tell me." She curled her lip, adding on a whisper, "Don't make me go on there."

"Excuse me." A baritone voice paired with a gentle tap on my arm had me automatically turning. Moving my hair behind my shoulder, I tacked on a polite smile, preparing for a fan or—worse—someone coming over to ask me about my callback this week. Instead, I came face-to-face with one of these bearded boys with whom Lina seemed preoccupied.

Inspecting him quickly—flower at his lapel, tux, brown beard, thick, dark lashes framing eyes that weren't hazel or blue but something in between—I felt my lips curve on their own. I recognized him. He was one of the groomsmen, which meant he might've been one of the brothers of the groom. At the church, he'd been sandwiched between a huge, blond-bearded Vikings-esque male and a young Matt Bomer-ish /specimen with neatly trimmed facial hair and blue eyes that glittered like diamonds.

I will admit, the men at this wedding had been quite a sight with their broad shoulders and capable-looking hands, seven of them standing at the altar like a buffet of mouthwatering masculinity. Or maybe a casting-call line for a lumberjack version of James Bond? Point was, even I—determined to be disinterested in men, romantic relationships, or any form of distracting entanglement—was not unaffected.

I'd been affected.

Squirming in the church pew as I'd sinfully devoured the assorted eye candy in the bridal party, I'd sort of started to understand why Sienna had initially decided to stay in this two-hardware-store small town. *But . . . to marry it? To be impregnated by it after knowing it for only six months? To trust it?* No. No way.

Just the thought of finding myself in a similar predicament made me break out in a cold sweat and gave me itchy palms. I'm positive I'd had nightmares similar to Sienna's present reality. And so, I worried for her.

But back to the dish of mouthwatering masculinity that had just tapped on my shoulder.

"Yes?" I asked smoothly, stepping closer in bold invitation. Boldness was my default. If I was going to be rejected, I liked to know right away.

Also, I'd decided earlier (after the Magic Mike lineup at the church) that I wasn't opposed to partaking if an interesting man-snack materialized. Someone outside of industry circles. A local. Beard optional. Someone who was obviously interested in me (since breaking things off with Harrison, I had a strict policy of never chasing my snacks) but who also wouldn't make tonight into a whole *thing*.

That said, I would not be having a one-night stand with a brother of my good friend's new husband. If this guy was one of Sienna's brothers-in-law, he was off-limits.

The guy gifted me with a smile that seemed real but also foreign on his face, making me think he wasn't a person who smiled often. "I'm Cletus Winston, Jethro's brother. Sienna has spoken of you with great esteem."

Well, darn. That's that. No "man-handling" this one. Ha ha! Get it? No *manhandling*.

And what a shame. Cletus Winston's formal tone paired with his southern twang reminded me of the accents in *Gone with the Wind*. Honestly, I'm always looking for an opportunity to be reminded of the love story in *Gone with the Wind*. I had strong feelings about the dynamic between Rhett, Scarlett, and that tepid vanilla pudding of disappointment, George Ashley Wilkes.

Anyway, I liked how this guy spoke despite his unfortunate hillbilly name. Sienna's husband's name was just as cringey. What had their mother been thinking? *Cletus? Jethro? Yikes!* Especially when there were so many other great, strong southern names, like Mason, or Walker, or Marshall, or Jackson . . . *or Rhett*.

"Sienna is the best," I said—because she was the best—and gave this Cletus person a second look. The man wore a tuxedo and wore it well, but he also looked like someone who stepped out of the pages of "Little Red Riding Hood" and yearned to wield an ax instead of a bow tie. He was good-looking enough under all that hair, but definitely not my type.

In case you haven't guessed, my type was a Rhett Butler—a man who wore a tux the way he did everything else: with ease, charm, and a flavor of self-confidence that trended more witty-sardonic than egotistical.

Cletus Winston, brother of the groom, stepped to the side and twisted slightly at the waist, gesturing over his shoulder, and apropos of nothing said, "My friend over there is a police officer, local law enforcement."

Bemused, I moved my attention to where he pointed and found another man about the same height as the unfortunately named Cletus. This one was less stocky, with decidedly less mountain-man vibes, and he was not in a tux. The man wore an extremely well-tailored three-piece suit in dark blue that fit his athletic body nicely. Quite, *quite* nicely.

My eyes lifted to the man's face, and I studied him. Good forehead; great hair, sunny blond with texturing spikes of brown and gold; straight, strong nose; symmetrical features; angular jaw in an oval face; close-cut beard that showcased the slight cleft in his chin. Extremely attractive, but not in the polished, too-perfect Holly-wood, metrosexual way that now super turned me off.

Presently, the officer's gaze of indeterminable color shifted from me to Sienna's brother-in-law and then back, his surprise unadorned by artifice. Obviously, the man had not been expecting to be introduced to me. Also obvious, he recognized me, knew who I was, and—based on where his eyes had just landed—he'd likely seen the topless scene in my latest movie.

Interested in me—check.

Not in industry circles—check.

Local—check.

And a police officer, eh?

"Oh? Is he?" I asked.

"He is." Sienna's brother-in-law nodded, his tone still formal. "And he's got handcuffs with him. Just FYI."

My attention cut back to this Cletus person, and I pressed my lips together to keep from laughing. *Oh, I see what's up.* "Thanks for the tip." I made a mental note to give Sienna shit about this.

While filming with Sienna two years ago, I'd joked once—just once —that I would be the first on set for the handcuffing scene near the end of the movie since being cuffed during sex always got me off, and she'd never let me live the stupid words down. I'd said it to shock her and anyone else listening at the time. Bravado always helped me conceal nerves and doubt. You know that old saying? *Fake it till you make it.*

But Sienna hadn't been shocked. She'd laughed like she thought I was a weirdo and sent me faux fur-lined handcuffs for my birthday.

"No problem. Have a nice evening," the brother of the groom said. And with that, he administered a bow of sorts and strolled away.

Well, okay then. That was weird.

Giving my attention back to the officer, I discovered he'd recovered quickly, his earlier surprise now mostly gone. He wore a small, secretive-looking smile, like he had *thoughts.* Like he found his friend's antics and the unexpected spotlight of my gaze amusing rather than uncomfortable or flustering.

His abrupt and successful recovery kinda sorta flustered me. I blinked. My boldness offset by confusion, I hesitated.

"Invite him over, or I will," Lina said after a protracted moment, surprising me as she came to stand at my shoulder.

"He has a beard." I made sure my tone sounded teasing as I continued to inspect this handsome stranger who didn't appear at all starstruck. "Are you sure you want to talk to one of these bearded lumberjacks?"

"But it's a short beard, and look at that chin, and that suit." She sucked in a breath through her teeth, making a slight hissing sound. "Mr. Police Officer aced the assignment."

I breathed a laugh and, shaking myself out of the strange self-doubt, crooked a finger toward Mr. Police Officer. He in turn cocked an eyebrow, placing a hand on his chest as though to say, *Who? Me?* innocence written everywhere except his eyes. Those were nothing but trouble.

A little flutter of excitement squeezed my chest, and I breathed through a sudden, unexpected burst of anxious energy. Nevertheless, I enjoyed the unanticipated crackling and warmth of electricity racing over my skin as our gazes continued to tangle across the room, and I crooked my finger again.

"This one is mine, Lina," I decided and said at the same time.

"Raquel. You know how I feel about chin clefts. Cary Grant has my heart forever. Rock, Paper, Scissors?" she pleaded.

I watched as Mr. Police Officer crossed the room toward me, took note of the smoothness of his gait, the graceful confidence of his movements. "Nope."

"Ugh. Okay, fine." At the edge of my vision I saw Lina cross her arms. "But if it doesn't work out with you two, I get dibs next time, if—God forbid—we ever come back here."

"Totally fine with me," I said, lowering my voice to add, "You know my rule."

"Since Harrison, the heart-breaking twatwaffle, never the same guy twice," she said under her breath just as the handsome man in blue made it to where we stood.

"Hi." Lifting my chin, I offered my hand to the stranger. "I'm Raquel Ezra."

"I know." He didn't smile, but his eyes, which I could see now were a deep, warm brown, danced. My heart stumbled over itself as he slipped his palm against mine, bringing the back of my hand to his lips. Brushing the barest hint of a kiss there, the texture of his beard teased my knuckles. Both sent lovely, spiky shivers up my arm and to my fingertips. "Jackson James. Pleased to make your acquaintance."

Jackson James? Now that was a name I could appreciate. Part of me, the seriously goofy part, wanted to respond with *Charmed, I'm sure.*

I forced myself to hold his gaze until he released my hand, and only then did I turn to Lina. "This is Lina Lestari."

He shifted the brunt of his charm to Lina, and I drew in a silent, steadying breath. *Okay, settle down Rae. Play it cool. Be cool. Be who he expects you to be.*

"I'm a big fan, Ms. Lestari. It's an honor."

These statements pulled a smile from Lina—no small accomplishment—and she offered her hand, which he took and shook gently.

12

Lina squeezed his hand tighter and shuffled a half step closer. "I know who you are."

"*You* know who *I* am?" This seemed to surprise him, but he took her statement in stride, a small, skeptical grin blooming on his lips. He had nice lips, the bottom one much fuller than the top.

"I do," Lina said. "Your sister is, uh, Janet. Right?"

"Janet is my mother. My sister is Jessica."

Lina nodded quickly. "I met them yesterday. Your sister is hilarious. She's dating one of the Winston brothers? The one with the red beard."

"Yes. That's correct." The officer's eyes narrowed just a fraction of an inch, his voice a modicum tighter, but still a deep, delicious rumble.

Before I could process the subtle shift in his mood, Lina's smile grew dazzling. "Tell me something, Mr. Police Officer."

"Anything, Ms. Lestari," he responded immediately, using her hold on his hand to maneuver himself between us. "But I feel I must tell you, I'm a deputy sheriff. Though you can call me Mr. Police Officer if it pleases you."

His voice was nice. And his accent was *real* nice, very Rhett-like.

"Okay, deputy." Lina tilted her head to the side. "Can you tell me what a toboggan is?"

"I absolutely can tell you what a toboggan is. Just let me grab a water here . . ." Somehow he managed to free his hand from her grip, and in the next moment he reached behind me. His chest brushed against my shoulder while his proximity offered the faintest tease of his cologne, a warm, toasty blend of citrus, sandalwood, and . . . *Is that jasmine?*

My lashes fluttered as he withdrew, leaving the faint impression of his scent behind, and my mouth felt dry and useless. *God, he smells good.* I loved me a good-smelling man. There was nothing on earth like it. Three things in life had no substitutions: a perfectly roasted marshmallow; the first cool, crisp day of fall after a long, hot summer; and the closeness of a warm, good-smelling man.

Don't mess this up, Rae.

Okay, look. I'd been in a self-imposed dry spell for over two years. Yes, my career came first, and any prolonged involvement with a man right now would only serve to distract me from my goals, ambitions, and meticulously crafted plans, because men could not be trusted. Period. I had to keep my eye on the prize, but that didn't mean I wasn't thirsty for something delicious.

Don't you ever get thirsty?

That's what I thought.

So, assuming I could keep my inner oddball in check, and he continued to press all my buttons without trying, and he was interested—which I was eighty-five percent certain that he was—*and* he didn't say or do anything to reveal himself as a tepid vanilla pudding of disappointment, chances were really good.

The sexy officer straightened, his eyes dark and hooded as they met mine, that wonderful spark crackling between us. But then, giving his gaze back to Lina, he said, "A toboggan is a hat."

I laughed, barely avoiding a snort, but I did wrinkle my nose as I spoke without weighing my words, "No. Don't listen to him, he's pulling your leg. It's not a hat."

The deputy glanced at me out of the corner of his eye, his gaze striking me as both hot and sharp, though his tone was conversational. "Yes, it is a hat."

"No." I faced him fully, my neck heating. "It's a sled."

He gave me the entirety of his attention, his forehead lined even as a small smile spread over his features. "A toboggan is a knit hat, Ms. Ezra."

I shook my head, now grinning uncontrollably for reasons unknown. "You are wrong, deputy. It's definitely not a hat."

He pursed his lips, his right eyebrow rising as he watched me with eyes that still felt sharp and hot, but now also assessing. "All right. How much do you want to bet?"

"Bet? You want to bet me that a toboggan is a hat?" Little did he know, I loved to bet. I loved games—chess in particular—but only ever when winning was a sure thing. Everyone but Lina knew a toboggan was a sled. Maybe he wanted to lose a bet with me?

His eyebrow hitched higher, and a faint shadow of challenge squared his jaw. "Yes, ma'am."

A wonderful little thrill, a spike of something hot and promising ignited low in my stomach at how he'd said the word *ma'am*.

Still grinning, I crossed my arms beneath my chest, careful not to spill my water. "Fine. What are the terms?"

His cognac eyes brightened and moved over me as he rubbed the close-cropped beard on his jaw. "How about, if I'm right—if a toboggan is a knit hat—then you let me show you around Green Valley."

"And if a toboggan isn't a knit hat?" I lifted my chin, deciding not to mention that my flight tomorrow left first thing in the morning; if he wanted to show me around, it would have to be right now. Regardless, it didn't matter, because a toboggan was a sled, not a hat.

15

He shrugged like it didn't matter, apparently certain he was right, even as his gaze grew in twinkly intensity the longer it held mine. "Name your price."

"If I'm right, then—" I paused, needing to swallow.

The side of his mouth hitched, such a flirty little curve, and my stomach erupted in butterflies. No lie, I hadn't felt anything close to this since Bryce Littleton's soccer ball landed on my lap freshman year of high school. He'd been a senior, experienced, and very, very hot. I'd been . . . none of those things. But the soccer star had winked at me and that simple action had detonated my first lust explosion, just like what I was feeling now.

Bryce Littleton had also turned out to be one hell of a good time. In truth, he'd been the only hell of a good time I'd ever had. No one else had come close.

Decided, I reached up and curled my fingers around the deputy's tie, slowly tugging it and him toward me as I leaned forward and, hoping my bravado made me sound badass instead of ridiculous, whispered in his ear, "If I'm right, then you—"

Lina thrust her phone at my profile, announcing, "He's right. A toboggan is a hat."

I flinched back, turning to face her, but didn't release his tie. "What?"

"I internet-ed it. It's a sled *and* a hat. But the bet was that a toboggan *isn't* a hat, so you lose." She wiggled the phone, a smirk on her purple painted lips. "Guess you're getting that VIP tour of Mayberry."

PART II

"Between two evils, I always pick the one I haven't tried before."

— MAE WEST

"*I* can't believe you people call a hat a toboggan," I muttered dumbly.

His lips curved, but then he quickly suppressed the smile, clearing his throat. "We're here."

"Here?" I peered out the windshield, having no idea where *here* was.

I'd been so confused that people in Tennessee called a hat a toboggan and hadn't said much after Lina declared him the winner. She'd cheerfully—well, cheerfully for Lina—steered us out of the tent, informing him that I would be leaving first thing in the morning, so the tour would have to start now.

Nor had I said much on the short drive over to wherever we were. My bravado had failed me. In this guy's quiet, steadily calm presence, I couldn't think of anything *to* say. Other than asking me if I was cold and offering me his jacket, he hadn't said anything either. I'd accepted the offer, and this might've been my fatal mistake because it smelled like him and made my insides warmer than my outside.

Cutting the engine of his truck, he exited the driver's side. Meanwhile, I unclicked the seatbelt and sighed, telling myself to speak as little as possible. If I didn't speak, I couldn't insert my foot. I would be aloof and mysterious. Except he was being quiet and mysterious, and we couldn't both be the aloof/quiet and mysterious one!

This was why I liked getting down to business without delay or discussion.

I couldn't tell you what kind of truck he drove. A big white one, and at least forty years old by the looks of it. The interior was clean, but the seat was one long bench instead of two buckets.

Oddly enough—and this might've been another reason why I'd remained mostly silent during the drive—the truck reminded me of Bryce Littleton's truck, the one in which I'd handed over my V-card. *Is the universe trying to tell me to call Bryce Littleton?*

I didn't think so.

Last I'd heard, Bryce had taken over his father's farm and married an office manager from Cleveland. That was four years ago, right after I'd moved to Los Angeles and started dating Harrison. *And that would make him, what? Twenty-six now?*

My hot deputy tour guide opened the passenger door just as I'd reached for the latch. That secretive little smile hovering behind his eyes and lips, he offered a hand to help me down, which, after a brief hesitation, I accepted.

Instantly, a shock of disorienting heat traveled up my arm, and I blurted, "How old are you?"

"Old enough," he said easily, his eyes moving over me like my question amused him.

"Seriously. How old?" I found my footing on the sidewalk and withdrew my hand.

"Twenty-six."

Twenty-six. Same age as Bryce.

"Did you play soccer in high school?" My chest felt tight.

He seemed to debate the question as he shut my door. "I did play soccer in high school, senior year. Why?"

"No reason." I twisted my fingers.

This was weird, right? Mr. Police Officer and Bryce Littleton didn't look anything alike, but the similarities were weird. Both from a small town, both drove an old truck with a big bench seat, both played soccer, both were three years older than me, and both were the only two guys who'd ever made me feel tongue-tied by saying nothing at all.

"Were you very popular? In high school?" I fell into step beside him as we strolled down the sidewalk, reprimanding myself for asking so many questions. How could I be perceived as aloof and mysterious if I kept talking?

He slipped his hands in his pants' pockets. "Not really."

So, that's different.

I felt myself relax just a wee bit, enough to curtail the urge to question him about whether his family owned a farm. At this point, I finally took note of our surroundings and realized he'd taken me to a quaint and deserted downtown. "Where are we?"

"Your friend mentioned you only have tonight for a tour, and we left before dinner. I thought you might be hungry."

"Well, that's thoughtful of you, deputy," I said, trying for flirty.

That secretive smile made another appearance. "I aim to please."

"Do you?" I bumped his bicep with my shoulder, feeling emboldened—finally. "How long is this tour going to take?"

He seemed to study me before answering, "Not too long."

"Not much to see in Green Valley?"

"Plenty to see, but I can't give you the full tour and get you home at a decent hour."

"What about an indecent hour?" AH HA! There she is. *I'm back in business, baby!*

He chuckled, a rumbly, masculine sound, his deep-set eyes dancing. "What are you hungry for?"

"What are my options?" I surveyed the street. It was just after 4:00 PM, but no one seemed to be out and about. All the shops looked closed.

"Sandwiches, soup, salad." He halted in front of one of the closed storefronts and withdrew a ring of keys. Words painted on the glass read, *The Sandwich, Soup, and Salad Stop.*

"But it's closed." I pointed to the closed sign hanging on the door.

"I have a key."

"Officer, do you own The Sandwich, Soup, and Salad Stop?"

"I do not. But I know the owner and she won't mind if we grab a bite to eat. If none of those appeal, I also know the owner of the Café on the Corner, and they have muffins and such from the Donner Bakery."

I glanced over my shoulder and then back to him. "You have a key to the café too?"

"I do."

Turning my head from side to side, I surveyed the shops along the sidewalk and spotted a hanging wooden sign for a place called Utterly Ice Cream Parlor. "What about the ice cream place?"

"You want ice cream?"

"Do you have a key?"

"Yes."

My lips parted as curiosity momentarily eclipsed my desire to be aloof and mysterious as well as my brash and bold instincts. "Everyone just gives you a key to their shops?"

He seemed to take my questioning in stride. "Not everyone. I don't have a key to the dulcimer shop, but my father does."

"Does he own it? The dulcimer shop?" I had no idea what a dulcimer was.

"No."

A nagging suspicion had my heart beating faster. "What does your father do?"

"He's the sheriff."

"And you're a sheriff's deputy," I murmured.

Bryce Littleton was a farmer with a farmer father. *What is going on?* Was this guy the Bryce Littleton of Green Valley, Tennessee? Did every small town have one?

"It's not so unusual in these parts for families to all be in the same line of work." He gave me his closed-mouth smile, one side of his lips pulling higher than the other, his eyes twinkling down at me. "Most of the Leffersbees, for instance, are in banking. The Donners run the lodge and have for generations. The Monroes are in construction—well, most of the brothers."

I supposed that was also true where I grew up. The people who stayed after high school tended to work with or for their families, in general. Or in the same line of work.

The flutter of disquiet lessened. "And your people enforce the law?"

"That's right." He confirmed with a single nod, his voice quiet and steady. "It's not so strange, if you think it over. Aren't there dynasties in Hollywood? Barrymores, Fondas, Smiths?"

Well, look at him. Pretty *and* smart. "Good point," I conceded, unable to stop my slow-spreading smile. He really was very pretty.

"So where are we going?" he asked, shifting his weight to his left foot and tilting his head, his eyes still on me. "The Stop, Corner Café, or Utterly Ice Cream?"

"I . . ." Reluctantly, I tore my attention from his gorgeous gaze, surveying the small downtown once more. "I guess, uh—"

Quick! What is sexy to eat? Not sandwiches. I didn't want chipmunk cheeks while chewing. Not soup. What if he slurps? That'd be a dealbreaker. And not salad; dressing is always a hazard. A muffin? No.

Too bad there weren't any banana stores around here.

"Ice cream," I said finally. Licking was good. *Perfect.*

"You want ice cream for dinner? In late November?"

"Whenever possible—" I winked at him "—I like to skip straight to dessert."

"Ice cream it is." He grinned.

Nailed it.

* * *

"We're stopping?"

"Yep." He nodded.

I frowned, gauging how far we were from the flow of traffic—not that I'd seen any other cars on the twisting, two-lane highway. He'd backed us onto what I assumed was a side shoulder and directly into the tree line. Just the hood of the car was visible from the road, and only if someone was really paying attention. The cab and truck bed were surrounded by brush and trees.

"We can stop here?"

"Yes."

"Uh, why are we stopping here?"

"We're just above Milton Overlook," he said, like all my questions would be answered by these words.

We were the only car pulled off the road, and it didn't look like much of an overlook. "So people pull off here to see a view?" Redirecting my attention behind us, I winced at the sun, low in the sky, coming in directly through the back window.

"Don't look back." He checked his watch. "It's not time yet; we're early. Give it another five minutes."

"We're early for an overlook?" I made a face without thinking, scrunching my nose. "Does the view put on a show? Are these hills alive with the sound of music?" *SHH! RAE! Stop talking. No more* Sound of Music *jokes.*

I braced myself for his reaction to my goofiness, but his eyes seemed to smolder as his lips tugged. He took his time, gazing at me like it was one of his favorite pastimes, before answering, "Something like that," in his deep, quiet southern drawl.

I bit the inside of my cheek to keep from saying something else stupid, like, *I do declare, Mr. Deputy. Your quiet, confident ways have me positively in raptures,* even though the words weren't far from the truth. My head felt dizzy, and I had to think he possessed some sort of sexy-voodoo magic. The recipe of him taken all together (that I'd seen so far) seemed unreal, too good to be true.

And yet everything about this guy felt entirely authentic.

He hadn't even looked at his phone. Not once. I couldn't remember the last time I'd been in someone's company—especially not for this length of time—without them at least glancing at their phone, checking their messages or recent likes and comments on Instagram.

Attention flickering over me, he reached behind us and pulled out the cooler where our ice cream resided. It was more than just a cooler, as I'd learned after he scooped a mint chocolate chip for me and double chunk cherry for himself. It was an ice cream cone carrier cooler, complete with cone-shaped holders and a power cord that plugged into the cigarette lighter of older model cars. I'd never seen anything like it.

Straightening in the seat, I hooded my eyes and put on my best sexy lady voice. "So, breaking into ice cream shops downtown and an overlook? Where else are you taking me on my grand tour of Green Valley, deputy?"

"This is it."

Really? "Really?"

"We've only got this evening, and most everyplace is closed due to folks being at the wedding, so I picked my favorite place that's close by and accessible." He checked his watch again and then twisted in his seat, obviously looking for something.

"I see." I inspected the tree branches pressed against my window. "This is one of your favorite places?"

He laughed lightly, his hand moving to the driver's side door latch. "I promise this won't disappoint, but next time you come to town, I'll take you all around. Hold on a sec."

Bringing the ice cream cone cooler with him, the deputy shoved his door open and hopped out, leaving me alone in the cab. He pushed past the trees, and I watched his progress until the beam of sunlight behind me made it impossible.

Facing forward, I listened to a series of doors or compartments being opened and closed, felt the truck shift and jostle like he'd jumped into the truck bed, and I contemplated the fascinating subject that was Mr. Jackson James, sheriff's deputy.

He didn't seem at all nervous, nor had he been brash and bossy, and this was unusual in my experience. I'd assumed if things progressed tonight, he would either be another fumbler with shaky, sweaty hands or a cocky, dominant type. Fumblers with shaky, sweaty hands and cocky, dominant types were basically the same guy in the sack and seemed to be the only kind of guy interested in me.

They expected me to do everything—play a role, be a fantasy—and when I did anything at all, they came in sixty seconds. At first, I was okay with this since they seemed happy *and* they'd always go down on me after, which used to be one of my favorite things. Plus, you better believe I made them work for it.

But after so many encounters of the same flavor, I started missing real sex. Eye contact. Touching. Foreplay. Friction. Heat. A man who lasted longer than it took my manicure to dry.

But this guy . . .

Checking my makeup in the mirror, I examined the reflection staring back at me and wiped my hands on the short skirt of my dress, worrying that if things did progress between us, I might be the fumbler tonight.

A sound yanked me from my reflections, and I closed the mirror, turning in my seat just in time to see him draw even with my door. He'd put on a brown jacket, part of his deputy uniform from the looks of it, and pulled open my door, holding back the branches and underbrush.

"Hey. It's time. Come with me." Once again, he held out his hand and, once again, I hesitated a split second before accepting it. No longer surprised when a shock of heat ran up my arm at the contact, I unthinkingly returned his small, intoxicating smile and forgot for a moment where we were, and maybe who I was.

He stood between me and the grabbing branches—ensuring they didn't catch on my hair or my dress, or scratch my skin—until we abruptly cleared the trees and encountered a cliff, beyond which was a sky painted in the colors of sunset while gauzy mist cradled between emerald green mountains.

"Oh . . ." I breathed, my eyes looking everywhere, absorbing the insane levels of beauty. A gust of wintery wind blew my hair back from my face and I blinked against it, turning my head slightly.

"Let's get up here," he said, leading me to the open tailgate. Bracing his hands on my waist, he lifted me up onto a cushy blanket he'd laid out.

Splitting my attention between the breathtaking view and my breathtaking companion, I watched as he climbed up beside me, sitting so close our thighs pressed together, knee to hip. He pulled a soft and fuzzy blanket from somewhere behind us and draped it over our laps.

Then and only then did he unzip the cooler and offer me my ice cream. "Here you go, gorgeous."

"Thank you," I said on autopilot, admiring the diffused light provided by the sunset and how it teased over his lightly tanned skin, reflected in his rich brown eyes, and glinted off his golden hair.

Sitting so close, I marked details of him that hadn't come into focus until now, and the sense that he was real and yet unreal at the same time crashed over me. Like a wave. Or being thrown off a cliff. He was really just too alarmingly pretty. And big. And strong. And dreamy. That's it—that's the word. He was dreamy.

He's a fantasy.

I breathed a laugh at the thought, at the irony.

"What's funny?" he asked, looking interested.

"Oh, I was just—uh—wondering . . ." I focused my eyes on my ice cream cone, but not my attention. My thoughts were chaotic, scattered. This was so weird. Everything about this was weird.

He bumped my arm lightly. "Ask me anything. But I warn you, there's not much to tell."

Ugh! And he's humble too?

I didn't know how to keep pretending with this guy. So I asked the first thing that came to mind, giving up all pretense of being aloof and mysterious for the moment. "Given this spectacular scenery, I understand why this is one of your favorite places. But where else, what else, is on your list? Where else would we go, if we had more time?"

"Well, first, I reckon I would ask what you like. Waterfalls? Prairies with wildflowers? Historical sights, hiking trails, picnics, views?"

He . . . he wanted to know what I thought? What I wanted?

I twisted my lips to hide the flutter of anxiety in my stomach, and I couldn't decide if it was the pleasurable kind of anxiety, or the bad, alarming kind. *It's both, and that makes it worse.*

The sudden impulse to sabotage this—whatever *this* was—by unleashing my true, weirdo self urged me to say, "I love to fish."

"You do?"

"I love to sit in a small boat in the sun and drink beer all day while shooting the shit. I don't even mind hooking the bait." I peeked at him, gauging his reaction. He didn't seem at all put off by this infor-mation. *Maybe I've been in LA for too long?* At a Hollywood party, admitting my love for fishing would have gotten me laughed at and labeled an "Elly May."

I hadn't understood the reference the first time it had been applied to me, so I'd looked it up. Elly May Clampett had been the earnest, uncouth daughter in the popular 1960s TV show *The Beverly Hill-billies.*

But the deputy seemed interested. Encouraged, I went on, "Fishing is probably one of my favorite things to do, right behind board game night, camping in a tent, and when my friends let me do up their face with whatever makeup I have on hand."

He unleashed a wide, pleased grin, but he might as well have released a kraken. I was stunned. *Stunned.*

His smile. Holy Moses, his smile was unreal, but it wasn't perfect. His teeth weren't quite perfectly straight—they probably had been at some point, right after braces, but not anymore—his lips pulled higher on one side than the other, making his grin crooked, and his eyes were nearly lost behind his brow and high cheekbones. But all these imperfections just served to make it—and him—absolutely perfect.

He leaned back, giving me the sense he wanted to get a better look at my face. "That all sounds awesome. My sister used to practice her makeup skills on me, since it was just the two of us."

I blinked at him, working to disguise my alarm. He'd reacted to my oversharing in the exact opposite way I'd expected, but I guess that made sense if I stopped to think about it. He was a small-town guy; he probably loved to go fishing.

I quietly sucked in a breath to steady my heart as it climbed to my throat.

Maybe . . . maybe this was a bad idea. Maybe the Hollywood fumblers and dominant types were where I should be focusing my energy. But I'd never fully enjoyed myself with those guys, just like I'd never enjoyed visiting the zoo. A tiger behind a thick sheet of glass and regulated to an artificial environment lacked something essential. But there was a reason why people didn't go visit wild animals in their natural habitats. Wild animals are real; they are dangerous; there are consequences.

Somehow, I needed to get things back on track, or I needed to escape this wild, real creature in his natural habitat.

"So, fishing. Got it," he said, as though adding fishing to this fictional agenda. "We have Bandit Lake for that. But in the evening, we'll go to the Front Porch for dinner, and after that, the jam session."

"Jam session?" I eyed my ice cream cone and then brought it to my mouth for a quick lick, needing something to do so I could get my brain house in order. "You get together and make preserves?"

He laughed, another big smile, and my heart reminded me again that his smile was wonderful. "Music. A bunch of local musicians get together and improvise."

"Do you play any instruments?" I licked a drip of mint chocolate chip from the back of my hand, not really tasting it. *Focus, Rae.*

"I used to. But I was never very good. Not like the folks who play at the jam sessions. They're the real deal."

More humility. My heart pinged, my neck hot.

"Professionals?" I asked, sighing my despair. Why is humility so attractive?

"I wouldn't say that exactly. But they all have natural talent and are quite good."

"But you're not good?"

"Not at that, no."

"Hmm." I licked my lips of residual ice cream, peering at him from the corner of my eye.

"What?"

"It's just strange, admitting you're not good at something." I bit into the scoop of ice cream.

He seemed to think my words were amusing. "Folks where you come from are good at everything?"

"No. But in Hollywood, everyone thinks they're the best at every-thing. And even if they don't think they're the best, they pretend they are. It's all a big game." A game I was usually quite skilled at playing, unlike this game.

"You like the game?" he asked, his tone distracted, and this brought my attention back to his face. I found his eyes hazy, affixed to my lips.

That's right! The ice cream cone.

Bringing the scoop to my mouth, I gave the side and top a swirling lick, watching his expression the whole time. "I do, actually," I said sexily (*sexily* being one of the funniest and most awkward words in the English language, but you get my point), and then licked my lips, slow and careful.

His eyes flared but remained on my mouth. "What are you doing?"

"Is it working?" I bit my lip, trying to appear coy and tempting.

The deputy's mouth curved, his eyelids drooping. "Depends. What are you doing?"

"Trying to make you hot by licking my ice cream cone."

He still studied my lips. "Mmm," was all he said, a low rumble from his chest.

I couldn't read him, so I asked, "It's not working?"

"Oh, no. It's working." He gave me a quick flash of teeth, his voice pleasingly gruff. "Let's see if this does something for you."

And then—and please, if you are easily shocked, brace yourself—the man let loose his tongue, licking his own two scoops in a startling display of control, skill, and WITH THE LONGEST TONGUE I'VE EVER SEEN!

Ever.

Ever in my whole life.

I grabbed his arm, turning completely toward him. "Oh my God!" I'd been mistaken. His smile wasn't a kraken; his tongue was the kraken.

He chuckled, looking—if you can believe it—a little shy.

Unthinkingly, I grabbed his face. "Show it to me again," I demanded.

He laughed harder but complied, his tongue slipping past his teeth all the way out to curl upward. His long tongue. His very, very long tongue. And it was not at all weird or freakish or unattractive because it was in perfect proportion and looked totally normal, just really, really long.

My breath shuddered out of me and then hitched. "You have a—a very—"

"Long tongue," he said, grinning. Maybe he found my reaction to this news funny? I didn't miss the faint hint of pink on his cheeks.

Oh no. He's adorable. Sexy, humble, adorable, calm, steady, bedroom eyes, kraken tongue. This was the worst.

"Yes. Yes, you do." I released his face and swallowed a rush of saliva, suddenly wanting to suck on his long tongue. "How is—how is that possible?" I didn't care that my words were breathless and I was making a complete fool of myself.

He shrugged. "Don't know. I was born with it." He licked his lips, just a quick flick.

Meanwhile, my eyes dropped to his mouth as I waited for another sighting. "I think you won this game."

"Were we playing a game?" He sounded both confused and pleased.

Thoughts burst forth unchecked. "Yes. I always play games, and I rarely lose. I have to hand it to you, deputy. You won that round fair and square." My face was flushed. Actually, everywhere was flushed, but not from embarrassment. I was flushed with anticipation. With want. With lust.

"Oh yeah?" He tilted his head to the side, watching me and whispering, "What did I win?"

"Whatever you want," I said, my stare back on his mouth.

I thought I could seduce him and keep things tidy, I thought I could be his fantasy, I thought I'd been in control. I was not in control. Whatever this was—this pull, this heat and energy—I'd never felt anything like it. Not with anyone. He won. I surrendered.

"Whatever I—whatever I want?" His words were halting, like they'd tripped over that glorious, huge tongue of his.

"Yes!" I nodded emphatically. I wanted him. Badly. So I think I can be forgiven for blurting, "But preferably something involving your tongue."

Lifting my eyes so he would see I was serious, our gazes clashed, a jarring bolt of something hot and electric racing down my spine, twisting low in my stomach. He didn't look amused, and he didn't wear a smile. His eyes weren't dancing. They were intent, focused, and so very, very hot.

33

PART III

"It's tougher to be vulnerable than to actually be tough."

— RIHANNA

"I think . . ." he started, then stopped, his eyebrows pulling together. The deputy licked his bottom lip and drew it into his mouth to nibble on it. The movement seemed reflexive and thoughtful, artless. Which was probably why it got me so hot.

Abruptly, he blinked several times in quick succession and stood, tossing his ice cream cone away and giving me his back. His shoulders seemed to rise and fall on an expansive breath before he turned around, his secretive smile in place, his eyes not quite meeting mine. I began to suspect this smile I'd labeled as secretive might've actually been shy.

Before I could give this suspicion too much thought, he stepped closer and invaded my space, his stare fastened to my lips. "As I said—" he leaned forward, nuzzling my nose gently with his "—I aim to please."

35

I lifted my chin, expecting—no, aching for—a kiss. I felt his hand close around my wrist and slide to my fingers, prying them open and encouraging me to release my ice cream cone. He tossed it away, and I didn't even care. Sacrificing mint chocolate chip on the altar of sexy promise, the potential of his long tongue held me transfixed.

The fuzzy blanket slid from my lap, baring my legs to the cold air, and he shook it out and laid it behind me, bracketing my body with his arms as he did so, keeping inches between our lips. Finished with the blanket, he placed a palm on each of my knees and gently pushed them apart. He didn't step between them, but instead slid the backs of his fingers along my inner thighs to the scrap of lace between my legs, lifting my little skirt.

I swallowed reflexively, chasing my breath. He looked so certain, like he was following a script, like he knew *exactly* what to do. And here I was, just sitting there like a lump, doing absolutely nothing except watching this fantasy come to life.

"Are you cold?" he asked, his thumb circling me through the lace of my panties, making me shiver and pant.

"No. No." I shook my head, my words shaky. "Not at all."

His attention shifted to the suit jacket still covering my shoulders. On a wild whim, afraid he'd stop if he thought I was the least bit cold, I pushed off the jacket. And then, because I really didn't want him to stop, I leaned forward enough to untuck my dress from where I'd been sitting on the hem and whipped the stretchy black fabric over my head.

His lashes flickered, perhaps having trouble believing his eyes, and a breathy curse slipped past his lips. I'd surprised him, but his thumb never ceased its gentle torment at my center. I widened my legs.

"Take off your bra," he said, his words firmer than before, his eyes dropping to my chest. "I'd like to lick you there first."

Yes. Please.

Usually, I waited to release the girls until they could be revealed in a dramatic, high-tension, super-sexy fashion, with just the right lighting. And yes, I called my breasts "the girls" because to me they were amazing, and girls are amazing. I'd always loved my boobs. Maybe it's weird, but when I got myself off, I liked looking at and touching my boobs. I thought they were so hot. I loved them, and I hoped all women got as much enjoyment out of their girls. *Girl power.*

But at present, I didn't care about a dramatic reveal. With slightly trembling fingers, I unhooked my black lace bra and tossed it away, maybe down the cliff. Then I arched my back, offering myself, not missing the shaking breath he released as his gaze grew greedy, the first tangible signs that I might be affecting him the same way he'd been affecting me all afternoon.

I reached for him, but he evaded my hands, shaking his head. "Hands behind your back."

A new current of something powerfully seductive made my head spin. He sounded so authoritative, like someone who actually had the power to make such a demand. Which I supposed he did. How many times had he said those words as an officer of the law?

Without thinking, likely because he had me completely enthralled, I said, "Yes, sir," and obeyed.

Two lines appeared between his eyebrows, a hint of a frown, and I wondered what was going on in his head. But a second later, his expression eased, and he slid a hand from my thigh to my hip and stomach, around my side to the dip of my waist, his long fingers flexing on my lower back. His hands weren't shaking or fumbling; they were certain and sure, methodical, careful.

Meanwhile, I was on fire, restless, feeling needy, and I knew without a shadow of a doubt the moment any part of his bare skin or tongue or lips came in contact with the ache at the center of my body, I was going to come embarrassingly fast.

I tried to regulate my breathing, but I couldn't. How his eyes followed the path of his hands on my body, the way he licked his lips—another flick that looked reflexive rather than planned—as he bent his head to my chest, the sight of his mouth closing over my breast . . . it all robbed me of breath.

And then the hot, swirling, wet slide of his tongue against my nipple made me cry out. I arched my back, closing my eyes, my body trembling and tensing around absolutely nothing. I was in free fall, and I felt so empty. This was insane.

Fuck. I was going to come. I was going to come, and his touch was still just a light whisper between my legs. I sucked in a breath, working frantically to brace myself, pace myself. But then he withdrew his mouth, giving me just the sight of his tongue tangling with the hard peak of my nipple as his hand slipped unhurriedly into the waistband of my panties with sure, authoritative movements. My breath hitched, and he made this delectable growling sound in the back of his throat, the pad of his middle finger sliding between my folds and circling my clit once.

Just once.

Just fucking once!

And I came. I came, and I heard myself come, and I wanted to cringe at the helpless, high-pitched keening sounds I made, but I couldn't contemplate anything other than how badly I needed this, needed this pure fantasy of a man, with his certain movements and sexier-than-hell smiles.

I hadn't quite finished making a fool of myself, my orgasm not yet spent, when his hands began moving again, hooking into the waist of my underwear to pull them down. They left my body, then his mouth was back on my breast, his kisses hungrier this time, the suction harder. He palmed and massaged my other breast, pinching and twisting and just generally abusing my nipple in the best way possible, another growl escaping him as I gave a throaty cry.

My arms behind me started to shake, and so he wrapped one of his around my body, supporting me. I felt the muscles beneath his coat and shirt flex, squeezing me tighter. I was cold and hot, goose bumps all over, and my teeth chattered. But I didn't care because Deputy James was now kissing my stomach, and then lower, and then lowering himself, his tongue swirling and tasting my skin on his way down.

"Lie back." His order was gruff, and I was surprised when he followed it with a soft, "Please."

The please wasn't necessary. I was more than happy to do as I was told, but I did lift my head so I could watch him lift my legs and spread me wide and place a biting kiss on the inside of my thigh.

And then—oh mygod ohmygod ohmygod—he fully extended that glorious mouth muscle of his and he licked me exactly how he had the ice cream. When guys had gone down on me in the past, it had always been a slow, warm build over a long period, with a few misfires and adjustments. But not this time. This time it was all hot electricity and scorching shocks racing from my lower abdomen to my fingertips and toes.

I made more cringey and helpless high-pitched noises, my fingers grabbing the thick tufts of his golden hair, and he licked and licked

39

and licked, the hairs of his short beard a sharp, stinging contrast to the velvet of his tongue, the sounds he made positively and unapologetically indecent, and so mind-blowingly erotic.

I didn't want another orgasm, not yet, but I honestly had no choice. I had no control over the speed and force of my climax, especially not when he slipped long fingers inside me and hooked upwards, instantly finding and massaging my G-spot like someone had given him a damn map.

Insane. I felt insane. This was insane. He was magical. He was unreal. I cried out, and then my cries became growls and rough curses, my hips pivoting and jerking gracelessly until my entire body locked, every muscle involuntarily flexing as spasms of pure, incandescent pleasure tore me in half from head to toe.

I'd never locked up during an orgasm before. I'd always been in control of my body and how it reacted to manly ministrations or my army of vibrators. So this—losing control of my limbs and the sounds I made—was a new and bewildering experience for me. It was like . . .

Well, it was like . . .

Possession.

That's what it was, like being possessed by blinding light and heat and pain and pleasure and feelings too large for my body. I was momentarily overwhelmed, unable to fully engage my mind, even when my muscles and joints finally unlocked and I could move them. I sucked in my first full breath in what felt like hours, and my body melted into a mass of intensely satisfied bonelessness. I then opened my eyes. I hadn't realized I'd shut them.

Blinking at the winter sky above me, I listened to my own breaths saw in and out, the rapid drum and thump of my heart. I listened to the sounds of twilight, the wind through the trees, the faint, distant call of a bird. I listened to Deputy James's slow kisses as he continued to touch me, move his mouth and hands over my body, caressing my hips, sides, arms, stomach, and breasts—like he still wanted to devour me, but slowly. I felt savored.

Swallowing against some foreign rising tide of emotions I couldn't name, I lifted my head and looked at the top of his. My fingers were still in his hair, and he was presently kissing my right breast, spending an inordinate amount of time tasting me there, giving me the sense he couldn't get enough. His hair was soft and thick, and I resisted the urge to pet it, sliding my hands down to his neck and into the collar of his jacket, but not into his shirt because he still wore his tie. This frustrated me. I wanted to feel his skin.

Actually, no. I more than wanted to feel his skin. I needed to feel him. I needed to be wrapped up and held tight. This odd urge to be held clogged my throat and made drawing a full breath difficult.

"Hey," he said, his lips moving from my clavicle to my shoulder. "Are you okay?"

I shivered, because it was cold and an instinct I didn't understand— and was frantically working to suppress—continued to demand his weight, his skin, his arms around me. But I wasn't going to ask.

"I am much better than okay," I said, my voice raspy, my throat hurting a little, and I felt compelled to add, "Sorry about . . ."

He bit the spot where my shoulder met my neck and then lifted his head when I didn't finish my thought. Dark eyes capturing mine. God, he was handsome. So handsome.

"What?" he asked, and I tried to ignore the heat of his palm where it rested on my hip.

"Sorry about being a screamer," I said, grimacing.

"I didn't mind." He smiled. Not a big one like before. And not that secretive-shy one I enjoyed so much. This one was new, and I didn't know what it meant because I didn't really know this guy.

And for whatever reason, this new smile made me feel shy and uncertain. Me. Raquel Ezra. Hollywood starlet and bombshell who had no problem with full-frontal titty close-ups. My heart beat a strange rhythm, slow and thick, and my neck itched, and my chest felt hot, and . . . *am I blushing?*

Oh God.

I'm blushing.

What did that mean? Am I embarrassed?

Yes. That is what is happening. You are embarrassed. Or you're self-conscious, which is embarrassment's irritating little brother.

I—I needed to do something to stop it. *DO SOMETHING RAE!*

I'll . . . Give the man a blow job. *Good plan.*

"Hey. Are you okay? You're shaking." His smile had waned by slow degrees as he stared down at me, and now his eyes looked soft and concerned.

Worried that my inner turmoil could be read on my features, I slid a smile in place along with a mask of confidence, and I reached for his belt buckle.

His eyebrows jumped, and the hand on my hip intercepted my fingers before I could make any real progress. "Hey—hey, wait. Wait a minute."

"Wait?" I moved my eyes up and to the right, like I was debating his request.

He reared back, huffing a laugh and removing himself from the radius of my grasping hands. He also lifted and placed a corner of the fuzzy blanket over my body as he withdrew, covering me.

"You've got to be freezing. It's getting dark. We should—uh, we should go." He sounded entirely reasonable and even nodded at his own assertion, sparing me a quick, tight smile. "I don't want you to catch a cold, and you got that early flight."

Before I could react fully to these statements, he placed my dress and underwear on the tailgate next to my hip. "Here. Let me go pack up." He picked up the ice cream cooler and pushed his way past branches and shrubs for the cab of the truck, leaving me alone, like I might want privacy to dress.

Staring at my clothes, feeling unsteady and completely confused, I felt and heard the passenger side door open, the rustling of items, and other miscellaneous busy sounds.

Uh. Okay then. I guess he doesn't want a blow job.

What could I do? I put on my clothes, my brain a mess of confusion. What kind of guy doesn't want a blow job? My whole post-adolescent life, I'd been working under the assumption that it was a truth universally acknowledged. All men like blow jobs.

Maybe he just doesn't want a blow job from you. Frowning at the inkling that was quickly becoming a suspicion, I put the black dress on first, then my underwear, then I hunted for my bra, which I now regretted tossing haphazardly in a random direction. But you know what I didn't regret? That orgasm. Rather, to be more accurate, *those orgasms.*

If he didn't want anything in return, fine. I'd have him drop me off at my hotel and I'd take a hot bath and I'd cherish the memory of this evening for a long time. He didn't have to worry about me trying to make more out of this than a fun memory. I wasn't going to make demands or expect him to—

Ohhhhh! That's the problem.

I turned at the sound of him closing a door to the truck and watched him walk along the side, pushing branches out of his way. Waiting until he made it to the tailgate, I stepped forward and said, "You know, tonight, this is totally no strings."

He'd been reaching for the fuzzy blanket when I started talking, and his movements paused when I said *no strings*. Sending me a quick look I couldn't interpret, he nodded and folded the blanket. "Good to know."

"Okay. Good." I also nodded, strangely not feeling good. I felt compelled to add, "I just want to be clear. I have no expectations of you. None at all. This can just be two people having a fun time. Like—like fishing. This"—I pointed to the truck bed and then to my body—"you can consider what just happened here to be just as meaningful and recreationally enjoyable as fishing."

Not looking at me, he finished folding the blanket and hopped up into the bed of the truck. "Gotcha. Message received."

"So . . ." I glanced at his shoes and legs, still not feeling any better, and blew out an audible breath. "I can't find my bra."

He smiled, just a small one. "You, uh, threw it off the cliff."

"I did?" Setting my hands on my hips, I peered over the edge. "Huh."

"Yep. Just sling-shotted it right over."

"Oh. Yeah. Well." I was nodding again, working to keep my voice conversational. "Hopefully, whoever finds it can put it to good use. My great grandmother used old lace bras to strain her tea. She'd sew them into little tea bags—you know the ones with the fold-over tops? Where you spoon the tea leaves inside? As the song says, 'Ain't no party like my Nana's tea party.'"

I guess I'd decided to stop trying to hide my weirdness. The man had just dined on my body like I was caviar and cake and didn't seem to have any interest in me returning the favor. What was the point of pretending now? Our time together was apparently at an end.

"That's pretty clever," he muttered, stuffing the fuzzy blanket into a bin mounted to the truck bed. The cushy blanket I'd been sitting on during our interlude followed. Actually, I decided I would call it an inter-*lewd*, which felt a bit more comedic and therefore palatable given the last few minutes.

Hopping down, he landed on his feet like a cat and swiped something from the bed before shutting the tailgate. He then turned to me, his expression a warm neutral in the waning light, and crossed the short distance that separated us.

"Here," he said, settling his suit jacket around my shoulders, his smile soft. "You gotta be cold."

I eyed him, instinct wanting me to respond with something sassy like, *You want to come back to my hotel room and warm me up?* I couldn't quite form the words. He'd rejected me, right? When I'd reached for his belt and he'd pulled away, that was rejection. If he didn't want me, that was fine. I was fine. It was fine.

"I guess I'm a little cold," I said, just to say something, because he was still standing close. In the next moment, he slid his hands into the jacket, settling them on my hips, gazing down at me with those wonderful eyes.

Deputy James's lips parted, and he breathed out. I got the sense he was thinking, considering what to do next. Or maybe he didn't know what to say. Or maybe he didn't believe me, that this—tonight —came with no expectations.

"Listen, I meant what I said. This is one hundred percent no strings. I'm not—I leave tomorrow. And I have a rule about this kind of stuff. You don't need to worry about me."

"A rule?" He shuffled his feet, moving him closer, his hands inching around to my back. "What kind of rule?"

"I'm never with the same guy twice. There's something about the— the elegant tension of one-night stands, you know? Two strangers sharing their bodies but nothing else? If we have sex, you never have to worry about me talking to you after."

"You're talking to me now."

"Yes, but we haven't sealed the deal, have we? Once we have sex, that's it. You're dead to me."

His eyes narrowed but his lips parted with a half grin. "Excuse me?"

"You know what I mean. You're not *dead* dead to me. Like, if I see you in a Starbucks, I'm not going to think you're a ghost."

He laughed even as he pressed his lips together.

I plowed ahead, determined to get my point across. "If I see you, I'll say hi. But my life being what it is right now, my career has to come first. I have the rule—no repeats—and that keeps things tidy for all involved. Plus, it's fun. And people like to have fun. I like fun."

Like before, his grin waned, his gaze turning thoughtful as I spoke, and I could see he was considering me. "What are you doing now?"

"Right now?" I looked to my left and right.

"No." He breathed a light laugh, his fingers flexing on my back. "I meant, what are you doing for the rest of tonight?"

"I have no plans."

A mild frown arrested his features. He stared at me, his gaze intent, but said nothing. I stared at him in return, waiting, because I had no idea what this expression on his face meant. The moment seemed to go on and on, neither of us moving. My heart gave a little tug, a painful and sad spasm at the thought of ending our time together.

It felt premature. We'd left the wedding just a few hours ago. We still had time, if he wanted. *If he wants.*

At length, he opened his mouth, perhaps to speak, and so I said, "If you want, we can spend the rest of the night together. Doing things."

"Things?" His frown eased, but I felt reluctance in how he held his body, the tension in his frame. "What kind of things you got in mind?"

"I don't know. How about Vegas Chess?" As far as I knew, there was no such thing as Vegas Chess.

"What's Vegas Chess?"

"I'll teach you. It's a betting game." It was not a betting game. I'd just made it up.

He tilted his head to the side, narrowing his eyes. "Chess is not a betting game."

"It is. This version of it is." I nodded earnestly, the picture of wide-eyed innocence as I lied. "It's the origin of strip poker. For every pawn you lose, you have to take off a piece of clothing."

He grinned suddenly, like he couldn't help himself. "What happens if I lose one of my knights?"

"First base." My heart fluttered with anticipation and a scant bit of nerves. *Please say yes.*

His lips twisted. "What about the rook?"

"Second base." *Please say yes.*

"Queen?"

"Cunnilingus." *Please say yes!*

A sudden laugh burst from his lips, and he shook his head. "And if you lose your queen?"

I didn't think twice about lifting an eyebrow and saying, "Fellatio."

His eyes narrowed again, but I didn't miss the spark of heat. "Bishop?" he asked, his voice full of gravel.

I worked to hide the nervous energy clogging my throat and smiled sweetly, swallowing before leaning close to whisper, "Missionary."

PART IV

"A wise girl kisses but doesn't love, listens but doesn't believe, and leaves before she is left."

— ATTRIBUTED TO MARILYN MONROE

*H*e drove me to my hotel, walked me to my cabin, and left me at the door with a promise to return soon. I used the time to take a quick shower and change into black yoga pants and a white tank top. Since the good deputy had seemed mesmerized by the girls earlier, I decided to forgo a bra.

True to his promise, he returned a half hour later bearing a platter of veggies, meats, cheeses, and a bottle of wine, explaining that he knew the owner of the hotel—or rather, what he called the lodge. The food was from the restaurant kitchen and the wine was from the cellar, both of which he'd apparently felt free to raid.

He also had a chess board tucked under one arm and did not delay in setting up the game on the coffee table. In truth, until I spotted the chess board, I'd still been feeling uncertain about whether or not he actually wanted to be here with me tonight.

The entire platter of food and two glasses of wine later, Vegas Chess was now my favorite game, and I was no longer in doubt of the deputy's desire to stay. He wanted to be here. And the reason I knew for a fact that he wanted to be here was because he'd lost six pawns right off the bat, removing his jacket, shirt, tie, shoes, and belt, and grinned the whole time.

His rook was lost shortly after, and the game paused as I jumped to my feet and crossed to where he sat on the couch. Straddling his lap, I placed my hands on the back of the couch and giggled like a loon. I had no idea why I felt so giddy. Probably the wine.

"Are you ready to make out?" I whispered.

He settled his hands on my backside and squeezed, massaging me through my yoga pants. I loved how his hands held my body, like touching me was so natural, and something he truly enjoyed. "Why are you laughing?"

I grinned down at him, widening my legs and settling myself more fully on his lap. This made him clench his teeth, the muscle ticking at his temple. "I haven't made out with anyone since high school."

"What?" His eyebrows jumped. "We just—I just—"

"Oh, no." I rolled my eyes. "I mean I haven't *just* made out with someone since high school. Usually, I skip over all the good stuff and go straight to the other stuff."

"Like taking a queen or bishop?" He slid his hand up my back, using his fingertips to press me forward.

"Exactly," I said, my chin lifting as he sought my mouth. "Uh-uh. No kissing. Neither of us took a knight."

His gaze turned into a mock glare, his lips twisted as though to hide amusement. "All right," he said, overpronouncing the *t*, and then shifted me to the side so he could reach the board. He picked up his queen and moved her diagonally until she captured my knight, leaving his most valuable piece exposed to both my bishop and a pawn.

"Now come here." He pulled me back in place and then cupped my cheeks with his large palms, his eyes zeroed in on my mouth.

"Are you kidding? That was a terrible move. I'm just going to take your—*Mmm . . .*"

I never finished the thought because he captured my mouth, his lips a hot press. My head swam, my toes curled, and he held me still, breathing in through his nose. I expected him to deepen the kiss right away, but he didn't. He withdrew, his thumb caressing a line along my cheekbone before he returned for another press, angling his head to the side, playing with my lips.

My fingers fisted in the front of his shirt and I arched my back, shifting restlessly on his lap, wanting more. Yet he still kissed me sweetly, retreating a mere millimeter to brush his mouth softly against mine.

"You have amazing lips." His voice, just above a whisper, made my chest feel hot and tight and the rest of me feel needy.

I waited for him to add something suggestive like, *I can't wait to see them wrapped around my cock*, because why else would he compliment my lips? But the expected statement never came.

"They're perfect," he added, then nuzzled my nose before kissing me, pressing slightly harder. His hands returned to my ass, squeezing and massaging as his mouth moved and a grumbly sound reverberated in his chest.

I felt him, between my legs. I felt the hard, solid length of him, and so I rolled my hips, making him gasp. He wrapped his arms around my torso and licked at the seam of my mouth, imploring me to open. Happily, I obeyed, groaning my pleasure as he gave me his tongue and I finally got to play with it. And oh, let me tell you—it was magnificent.

We kissed and kissed and kissed, and I could not get enough of his mouth. Or his stroking hands. Or his strong arms. Or—when I finally had the presence of mind to lift up his undershirt—his stomach and sides. He felt so great, *so great,* and pretty soon my body took over, rocking against his concealed erection, searching for that lovely, exquisite friction.

"Fuck, Raquel," he said on a breath, lifting up my shirt to cup my breasts with both hands, the pads of his thumbs stroking back and forth over my nipples. "You are so fucking sexy."

Spikes of heat erupted all over my skin, little pinpricks, like an electric shock. "So are you, deputy."

"Jackson. Call me Jackson."

"Jackson."

"Wait—wait." He removed his hands from my chest, sliding them to my hips and holding me still even as his hips thrust upward. "Wait. Stop. I need a minute."

I stopped moving, though his request confused me. Why take a minute? Why not just ask me to help him out? Did he not *want* to come?

Pressing his forehead to mine, breathing hard, he gently cupped my jaw and sifted his fingers into my hair. Even though we were close, I could see he'd closed his eyes, scrunched them shut, his face screwed up as though in pain.

"Jackson. Let me help," I whispered, sliding my hands down the front of his body but not touching the button of his pants. The last time I'd made overtures, he'd withdrawn. I didn't want to repeat the same mistake.

He chuckled and exhaled a loud sigh. "I haven't taken your queen."

I twined my arms around his neck and studied him. All night I'd been admiring his face for being handsome, for being real, but presently I decided I also just really liked his face. He had a great face. Everything about it was great. And I liked looking at it.

"Do you want to keep playing chess?" I asked, my gaze lingering on the slight cleft in his chin, and then moving to the scrumptious fullness of his bottom lip. "Or do you want to do something else?"

He opened his dark eyes and was now studying me in return. "What do you want to do?"

Stay one more day.

I stiffened, blinked, frowned at the completely unbidden and unexpected thought. "I—" I shook my head. "I—uh."

I couldn't stay one more day. That would be absurd.

"Do you want to play chess?" he asked, his voice a low rumble. "I'll do whatever you want me to do."

At his words, my heart took off, and I blinked rapidly. *Stay one more day, Rae. What's the harm in staying just one more day? Think of all you could do with this man if you had a whole day. Maybe we could go fishing!*

I snapped my mouth shut and swallowed. There was no way I could stay one more day. I had a callback this week for a part I *really* wanted. I had meetings and lunches and rehearsals. I had a one-night-only rule for a reason. I never stayed. And why on earth would I want to stay here? I didn't belong here any more than I belonged in the town where I grew up.

Untwining my arms from his neck, I leaned away and rubbed my forehead. "You know, I think I had a little too much wine."

"You want some water?" He dipped his chin, likely trying to catch my eyes.

I climbed off his lap. "Yeah, I think I'll go grab some. Do you want any?"

"No, I'm good. Thank you."

I crossed to the bathroom but didn't shut the door, giving myself a stern, silent, and self-deprecating come-to-Jesus talk in the mirror during the time it took to fill a water glass and drink it.

Flipping off the light as I exited, I looked to the couch for Jackson, but I found him by the bed, buttoning up his dress shirt.

My heart jumped to my throat and I jumped into action. "What are you doing?"

He glanced at me, giving me an easy smile. "Getting dressed."

"What? Why?"

"It's getting late."

"But—but we didn't finish our game." I turned to the board and quickly claimed his queen with a pawn. "Ha! Look. You lost your queen."

His smile grew, but not by much. "You have an early flight. You should get some sleep."

I paced over to him but stopped myself from reaching out and grabbing his arm. "If you want to go, you should go. But I don't want you to go if you don't want to go. I'd—" I swallowed, for courage. "I'd like you to stay." *So much for not chasing my snacks.*

I caught myself, nearly frowning at the discordant thought, and assembled my features into a mask of friendly and flirty patience. And as we traded stares, I couldn't help but think, *This guy, he's not a snack.* Deputy James—Jackson—he was a meal. And not a Thanksgiving meal or a dinner party get-together. He wasn't someone to be saved for special occasions. He was an everyday favorite. No matter how many times or how often you partook, you always looked forward to the next time.

Jackson James is taco night.

He stopped buttoning his shirt and placed his hands on his hips. "I'll stay as long as you want," he said, peering at me in an odd way, giving me the sense he was trying to read my mind.

So I said what I was thinking, what I wanted. "I want you to stay all night. Why don't you—if you want, you could spend the night? We still have the chess game to finish. And then we could . . . go to sleep?"

Jackson's eyelids flickered, his gaze dropping to my mouth. I held my breath, waiting for his answer. *Please oh please oh please say yes.* I couldn't—wouldn't—stay in Green Valley for another day, but that didn't mean he had to leave yet.

Eventually, he gathered a deep breath and nodded, the side of his mouth pulling upward. "Okay. I'll stay. We'll finish our game, and then—" He stole a quick kiss, holding my gaze as he retreated. "We'll sleep."

* * *

Jackson was asleep.

For a while, I listened to him breathe, reveled in the feel of his warm, strong chest and arms bracketing my body, his hand on my leg, his leg between both of mine. A voice in the back of my head announced that if I actually fell asleep, this would be the first time I'd ever *slept* with someone.

My flight left at 6:10 AM, which meant I needed to be up and out of here by 3:45 AM at the latest. So why sleep at all? I only had—I checked the clock on the nightstand—two hours left. Telling myself that staying awake made the most logical sense, I gently covered his hand and brought it to my chest, placing his palm over my heart.

He didn't stir, and his breathing didn't change. I felt a little drowsy, but based on how quickly he'd succumbed to sleep, he must've been exhausted. I wondered how he'd spent his day prior to our introduction. Had it been busy? What time had he gotten up this morning? Did he have work tomorrow? I wished I'd asked.

Wake him up. Ask him. This is your last chance.

Or . . . maybe it wasn't my last chance. Technically, since we hadn't had penis-meets-vagina sexual intercourse, perhaps keeping in touch with Jackson wouldn't break my one-night-only rule. Maybe we could—

No.

I gave my head a subtle shake. We'd finished our game. He hadn't taken either of my bishops. If he'd wanted more with me, I'd given him every opportunity. We'd made out again—on the couch, on the bed—and then he'd gone down on me, saying it was only fair since I'd taken his queen, but his pants had stayed on the whole time.

That's right. He didn't even take my queen—despite my flagrant attempts to put her in harm's way—and neither of us had taken each other's bishops. He didn't give me an opportunity to swipe either of his priestly dudes, guarding them more diligently than even his king. Furthermore, he could've taken either one of my bishops several times. But he hadn't.

Why didn't he take a bishop?

I swallowed against a thickness in my throat, squeezing my eyes shut and sighing around an ache where his palm heated my skin. I was being silly, dumb. I didn't even know this guy other than he was a sheriff's deputy in a small town where his father was the sheriff, he looked good in a suit, and I would forever think of his tongue as the kraken. Also, he smelled fantastic and was easy to talk to and thought my lips were perfect and touched my body like it had been formed for his hands.

But other than that? Nada.

Stay . . .

Stirring, I huffed, pushing the ridiculous thought from my mind and opened my eyes. I glared at the clock and then reared back a scant inch. It was already 3:25 AM. My phone alarm would be going off in five minutes. How? How had that happened? I must've dozed off. My stomach twisted and a nauseous kind of discomfort climbed up my esophagus.

Shit.

Releasing a shaky breath, I removed his hand from my heart. Once more I debated waking him. Would he want me to say goodbye? Would he care? He'd been so cool with me. So undemanding and straightforward. He seemed to have a good time.

Worrying my lip, I disentangled myself from his body and skootched to the edge of the bed, turning to look at him over my shoulder after I flipped off my phone alarm, my heart pinging with a sudden and swift pain. *Ugh.*

I wanted to wake him. I decided I would. I would wake him and ask for his number, so we could keep in touch, if he wanted. And if he turned me down, so what? So. What. So I'd be . . . sad.

Pressing my lips together, I blinked back a rush of stinging moisture behind my eyes.

I'll be sad.

I tore my gaze from his handsome face and rubbed my forehead. God, what was I doing? What was I thinking? A sheriff's deputy? In a place named after a salad dressing? What? Hadn't I been the one scoffing at Sienna's choices yesterday during her lovely wedding? Yes. Yes, that judgy a-hole had been me. And nothing had changed.

Absolutely nothing.

So, no. I wouldn't wake him. I would leave because that's what we'd agreed. No strings. No problem. I'd forget him by tomorrow. Hell, I'd forget him by the time he woke up. *He'll forget me too.*

Spurred by that thought, I jumped from the bed and rushed to pack, swallowing convulsively because I must've been thirsty. For water. Whatever, it didn't matter. When he woke up, I would be long gone.

It didn't take much for me to assemble my things. I'd brought only the bare essentials and they all fit in my backpack. I dressed quickly in the bathroom, careful to be quiet, and soon I stood by the door, gripping my bag, ready to go. Turning over my shoulder, telling myself I should do one last sweep of the room, my eyes immediately landed on the gorgeous man asleep in my bed.

I still liked his face. A lot.

Before I could question the instinct, I lowered my backpack to the floor and tiptoed to the bed. Once there, I placed a careful knee on the mattress and bent forward, bracing a hand next to his head.

Staring down at him, memorizing the lines and angles of his hand-some face—wishing I could see his eyes one last time—I lowered the remaining inches and brushed a soft kiss to his lips, inhaling deeply. And then I leaned back, waiting, telling myself that if he woke up, I would stay for another day. *One more day won't make a difference.*

I waited. I counted to sixty. Then I counted to one hundred and twenty. And before my heart could react in some overly dramatic fashion—like plummeting in disappointment or twisting painfully—I straightened and turned, returning to the door. Blindly, I reached for the handle and gripped it, not allowing myself to feel torn.

Because I did need to go. There would be a car waiting for me by the entrance to the lodge. I had a flight to catch. I had a life in Los Angeles, a career I loved. We'd been on the same page from the start: No strings. No expectations. Just one night.

Just fooling around.

The End
(for now)

ABOUT THE AUTHOR

Penny Reid is the *New York Times, Wall Street Journal,* and *USA Today* Bestselling Author of the Winston Brothers, Knitting in the City, Rugby, Dear Professor, and Hypothesis series. She used to spend her days writing federal grant proposals as a biomedical researcher, but now she just writes books. She's also a full time mom to three diminutive adults, wife, daughter, knitter, crocheter, sewer, general crafter, and thought ninja.

Come find me -
Mailing List: http://pennyreid.ninja/newsletter/
Goodreads: http://www.goodreads.com/ReidRomance
Facebook: www.facebook.com/pennyreidwriter
Instagram: www.instagram.com/reidromance
Twitter: www.twitter.com/reidromance
Patreon: https://www.patreon.com/smartypantsromance
Email: pennreid@gmail.com ...hey, you! Email me ;-)

OTHER BOOKS BY PENNY REID

Knitting in the City Series

(Interconnected Standalones, Adult Contemporary Romantic Comedy)

Neanderthal Seeks Human: A Smart Romance (#1)

Neanderthal Marries Human: A Smarter Romance (#1.5)

Friends without Benefits: An Unrequited Romance (#2)

Love Hacked: A Reluctant Romance (#3)

Beauty and the Mustache: A Philosophical Romance (#4)

Ninja at First Sight (#4.75)

Happily Ever Ninja: A Married Romance (#5)

Dating-ish: A Humanoid Romance (#6)

Marriage of Inconvenience: (#7)

Neanderthal Seeks Extra Yarns (#8)

Knitting in the City Coloring Book (#9)

Winston Brothers Series

(Interconnected Standalones, Adult Contemporary Romantic Comedy,
spinoff of Beauty and the Mustache)

Beauty and the Mustache (#0.5)

Truth or Beard (#1)

Grin and Beard It (#2)

Beard Science (#3)

Beard in Mind (#4)

Beard In Hiding (#4.5, coming 2021)

Dr. Strange Beard (#5)

Beard with Me (#6)

Beard Necessities (#7)

Winston Brothers Paper Doll Book (#8)

Hypothesis Series

(New Adult Romantic Comedy Trilogies)

Elements of Chemistry: ATTRACTION, HEAT, and CAPTURE (#1)

Laws of Physics: MOTION, SPACE, and TIME (#2)

Irish Players (Rugby) Series – by L.H. Cosway and Penny Reid

(Interconnected Standalones, Adult Contemporary Sports Romance)

The Hooker and the Hermit (#1)

The Pixie and the Player (#2)

The Cad and the Co-ed (#3)

The Varlet and the Voyeur (#4)

Dear Professor Series

(New Adult Romantic Comedy)

Kissing Tolstoy (#1)

Kissing Galileo (#2)

Ideal Man Series

(Interconnected Standalones, Adult Contemporary Romance Series of Jane Austen Reimaginings)

Pride and Dad Jokes (#1, coming 2022)

Man Buns and Sensibility (#2, TBD)

Sense and Manscaping (#3, TBD)

Persuasion and Man Hands (#4, TBD)

Mantuary Abbey (#5, TBD)

Mancave Park (#6, TBD)

Emmanuel (#7, TBD)

Handcrafted Mysteries Series

(A Romantic Cozy Mystery Series, spinoff of *The Winston Brothers Series*)

Engagement and Espionage (#1)

Marriage and Murder (#2)

Home and Heist (#3, coming 2023)

Baby and Ballistics (TBD)

Pie Crimes and Misdemeanors (TBD)

Good Folks Series

(Interconnected Standalones, Adult Contemporary Romantic Comedy, spinoff of *The Winston Brothers Series*)

Totally Folked (#1)

Give a Folk (#2, coming 2022)

Three Kings Series

(Interconnected Standalones, Holiday-themed Adult Contemporary Romantic Comedies)